The Great Escape

Axel Feinstein

Look out for more stories
about Axel Feinstein!

The Great Brain Robbery

The Great Escape

Written by Alan MacDonald
Illustrated by Lizzie Finlay

■SCHOLASTIC

Scholastic Children's Books,
Commonwealth House, 1–19 New Oxford Street,
London, WC1A 1NU, UK
a division of Scholastic Ltd
London ~ New York ~ Toronto ~ Sydney ~ Auckland
Mexico City ~ New Delhi ~ Hong Kong

First published by Scholastic Ltd, 2003

ISBN 0 439 97850 5

Printed and bound by Nørhaven Paperback A/S, Denmark

2 4 6 8 10 9 7 5 3 1

CHAPTER 1
The Last Straw

"Today we're going to learn about flight," said Mr Crump, handing out pieces of paper to his class.

At the back of the class, Axel Feinstein stopped doodling designs for a remote-control teacher. This sounded interesting. Better than the usual spelling tests that Crump set them on Mondays.

"Let's start with an experiment," said Mr Crump. "Who thinks they can make a paper plane?"

"Wicked," said Darren. "What do we use?"

"Um, paper," Axel said. "I think that's why it's called a paper plane."

Mr Crump didn't explain to his class how to make paper planes. He wanted them to find out the hard way. The whole point of the lesson was to prove to his class that their teacher was a lot cleverer than they were. *Especially Feinstein,* he thought to himself. The boy was always correcting his spelling and making the class laugh. With his round

glasses and wild corkscrew hair, Axel
Feinstein looked harmless enough, but Crump
knew that Axel was trouble with a capital T.

Crump watched as Darren Blott wrestled
with his sheet of paper, folding it ten different
ways until it was roughly the size of a
postage stamp. Trudy was colouring her
piece of paper in stripes to match her
football shirt. Only Axel seemed to know
what he was doing. He scribbled
complicated diagrams in his notebook, then
swiftly began to fold his piece of paper.

"That's amazing, Axel!" said Trudy, when
he'd finished.

"Thanks," said Axel. "It's modelled on the Thunderbird jet, but I've made a few improvements. See, the rudder tilts right or left, and it's got these two elevators on the wings to give it extra lift."

"Brilliant," said Trudy, who had thought an elevator was something that went up and down in a shop. "Will it fly?"

"I don't know yet," said Axel. "I've never made a paper plane before."

"Time's up," said Mr Crump. "So, who'd like to try out their plane?"

He rubbed his hands together. This would be worth watching.

"What about Axel's?" said Trudy.

Crump ignored her. "Darren, let's see yours."

Darren Blott stood up and threw his grubby piece of paper into the air. He watched it plummet to earth like a stone. The rest of the class then tried to launch their planes. The air was full of fluttering and diving pieces of paper. Most of the planes didn't last long past take-off. Mae Li's flew for a few seconds until it nose-dived into Angela Price's forest of curly hair and never came out.

"We haven't tried Axel's plane yet," Mae Li reminded Mr Crump.

Crump pretended he hadn't heard. "If you want to see a real plane, take a look at this," he said. "She's called *Firebird*." He produced his own plane with a flourish. *Firebird* had taken Crump three months to build from a model aeroplane kit he'd spotted in a shop window.

The class were impressed. Axel stood up to get a better look.

"Fantastic, sir. Does it really fly?"

"Like an eagle," boasted Crump. "It's never been beaten."

"I bet Axel's plane could beat it," said Trudy.

"Not in a million years!" snorted Mr Crump.

That did it. The whole class demanded a flying contest. Axel's paper plane against Mr Crump's *Firebird*. Mr Crump smiled to himself. Secretly this was what he'd been planning from the very start, and Feinstein had walked right into his trap. No paper plane could be a match for *Firebird*. It was made of extra-light balsa wood and powered by an elastic band. For once Feinstein would be beaten.

"I'll be the judge," said Trudy. "Whoever's plane goes furthest is the winner."

Crump opened the classroom window wide. Axel drew his arm back. Crump wound the elastic band on *Firebird*'s propeller tight as a drum. Trudy counted down to take-off.

"Three – two – one... Go!"

Crump launched *Firebird* forward like a missile. In no time it was way ahead of Axel's paper plane. How far it would have flown they never discovered, because the next moment it smacked into the caretaker's shed. Crump watched helplessly as *Firebird* hit the window with a splintering sound and crumpled to earth.

Something white was still drifting across the playground. Axel's paper plane sailed on past the shed and landed on the playing field as gentle as a feather.

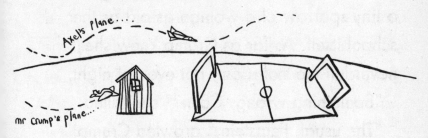

Axel's plane....

mr crump's plane....

The class mobbed Axel, cheering.

"The winner!" declared Trudy, raising Axel's arm in the air.

Crump ground his teeth. *Why?* he asked himself. *Why was it always Feinstein?*

At break Mr Crump sat in the staffroom, brooding over a lukewarm cup of tea.

Miss Peck sat down next to him. She was a tiny sparrow of a woman as old as the school itself. As far as Crump knew she never left the staffroom, not even at night.

"Something wrong, Colin?" she trilled.

"The usual. Feinstein," growled Crump.

"Ah," Miss Peck nodded. "And which one is she?"

"He! You know. Curly hair, glasses. Too smart for his own good," Crump said.

"Oh yes, Feinstein, such a dear child," said Miss Peck, who said the same about everyone.

"He should be locked up," said Crump. "This morning he wrecked my model aeroplane. Wrecked it!"

Miss Peck patted Mr Crump's hand, kindly. "I'm sure he didn't mean to."

"Oh, he meant to all right," fumed Crump. "Feinstein is out to break me. Sometimes I can hear his brain ticking away at the back of the class. Tick, tick, tick. Yes, I know what his game is, don't you worry."

Miss Peck wondered if Mr Crump needed a holiday. He was grinding his teeth and spilling tea on his trousers. She tried to change the subject.

"We had another bright girl once. Valerie Greengage. A dear child, but my goodness, sharp as a new pin."

"Really?" said Crump, stifling a yawn.

"Yes," said Miss Peck. "It was a pity she wasn't with us for long."

"Murdered by her class teacher?" asked Crump.

"Oh dear no, they sent her up to secondary school. She was only nine, poor lamb, but they felt she was too bright to stay with children her own age..."

Mr Crump set down his cold tea. He was suddenly giving Miss Peck all his attention.

"Can they do that?" he asked. "Send a nine-year-old child up to secondary school?"

"Well, not as a rule. It has to be a special case," said Miss Peck.

"Oh, believe me, Feinstein is a *very* special case," said Crump with a sinister smile.

"I was talking about Valerie..." said Miss Peck. But Crump had sprung to his feet and was already out of the door. A minute later he was knocking on the door of the Head's office. A happy tune was playing in his heart, and the words were: "Goodbye Feinstein, goodbye!"

CHAPTER 2
Hangem High

A week later a letter arrived through Axel's door. His mum read it while munching her toast and marmalade.

POTTER END PRIMARY School

Dear Mrs Feinstein,

I am pleased to tell you of a wonderful opportunity for your son Axel. You'll be delighted to learn that he has been offered a place at Hangem High School. I'm sure that Axel will be better suited to the higher level of education he'll receive at his new school. All the staff at Potter End (and especially Mr Crump) wish him all the very best for the future.

Yours sincerely

Mfudge

Mrs M. Fudge (Head Teacher)

Axel received the news as if he'd been sentenced to death. He didn't want to leave Potter End. Why were they sending him to a new school?

"Can't you just say no?" he begged his mum. "Just say I can't go."

"Don't be silly, Axel, it's a wonderful opportunity. It says so in the letter."

"But Mum! I'm happy where I am, I don't want to move schools."

His mum kissed him on the head. "I'm sure you'll love it. You're lucky to get a chance like this."

Axel's mum didn't know Hangem High, but she had a vivid imagination. She was already convinced it was one of those schools where rich, important people sent their children – a place where future kings and prime ministers rubbed shoulders.

The following Monday Axel trudged to school with his chin almost dragging on the pavement. Trudy had offered to accompany him as far as the gates.

"Why?" he asked. "Why can't I stay at Potter End?"

"If you say that once more I'm going to thump you," sighed Trudy.

"But it's not fair!" said Axel. "*You* don't have to change schools. Nor does Darren. Why me?"

"Obviously because you're such a brainbox," said Trudy. "I bet it's a school for boffins where they do amazing stuff like ... building rockets, or something."

Axel didn't look convinced. He didn't want to go to a school for brainy kids, he wanted to stay with his friends at Potter End. Trudy and Axel had been friends ever since Axel's first day at school. Axel relied on Trudy when he got into trouble – which for some reason seemed to be pretty often.

They'd reached the gates. Axel peered
through the tall railings to get a glimpse of
his new school. It was a crumbling, ancient
building made of mud-coloured stone. Vines
and creepers covered the walls and seemed
to be choking the life from it. Crowning the
roof was a bell-tower with a large rusty bell
which looked as if it
hadn't been rung since
Queen Victoria's
funeral.

Outside the
tall black
gates hung
a sign:

HANGEM·HIGH·SCHOOL.
HEAD TEACHER: MR.V.BATT

Just looking at the school made Axel feel anxious.

"They can't send me in there! It's like a prison," he protested.

"It doesn't look that bad," lied Trudy. (To be honest she'd seen graveyards that looked more cheerful.) "Anyway, Axel, you're bound to make new friends."

Axel peered doubtfully through the railings at the children. They were huddled in groups around the playground. None of them were running around or playing games.

"They're all bigger than me!" said Axel. "What kind of school *is* this?"

Trudy glanced at her watch. She hated to leave Axel, but she was already late for school herself.

"Sorry, Axel, got to go," she said. "I'll meet you here at home-time. Good luck!" She patted him on the shoulder and set off running down the road towards Potter End.

Axel watched her disappear with a sinking heart. Walking through the gates of a new school is never easy. It's even harder when you don't know a single person.

Axel was aware of countless pairs of eyes watching him as he crossed the playground. They were all staring. He wished someone would come over and say hello but no one did.

He came to a halt in the middle of the playground and stood there, studying his shoes. He'd never felt so small and lonely in his life.

He looked up to see a tall group of boys
watching him. One broke away from his
friends and came over. He had ink-stained
fingers and hair that
reminded Axel of a
hedgehog.

"I'm Ryder," said the boy. "What are you
here for?"

"It's my first day," said Axel.

Ryder snorted. "You? You're just out of
nappies!"

"I'm nine," said Axel.

"Nine!" repeated Ryder as if this was an
astonishing fact. "You're kidding me, right?"

He pointed at Axel's lunchbox. "What's in
there?"

"My sandwiches," said Axel truthfully. "And some crisps. And chocolate."

Ryder shook his head and tutted. "The Vampire won't like that."

"The Vampire?" said Axel, thinking he must have misheard.

"The head," said the boy. "Didn't you see his name on the sign? V. Batt. The V is for vampire. That's what everyone says."

"I don't believe you," said Axel uncertainly.

"Please yourself. Just warning you. If the Vampire catches you with chocolate he'll go ape."

"What shall I do?" asked Axel.

"I'll look after it," said Ryder. "You don't want to get in trouble on your first day, do you?"

"No," said Axel. He was about to open his lunchbox when he noticed Ryder turn and wink to his sniggering pals. Axel guessed it was a trick. Ryder wasn't being kind, he just wanted to steal Axel's chocolate.

"It's all right," said Axel. "I think I'll keep it after all." He snapped his lunchbox shut.

Ryder held out his hand. The concern had vanished from his voice. "Hand it over, shrimp," he said.

Axel hugged the lunchbox to his chest. "It's OK, thanks, I can look after it."

"But I say you can't." Ryder made a sudden lunge for the lunchbox. He grabbed hold of it but Axel didn't let go. He held on stubbornly.

"Get him, Ryder!" shouted the other boys. "Flatten the little shrimp!" They were closing in, making a circle.

Axel came to a swift decision. He didn't stand a chance against four or five boys twice his size. One chocolate bar was a small price to pay for getting out alive. Without warning, he let go of his lunchbox. Ryder wasn't expecting this change of plan and catapulted backwards into his friends, still holding on to the handle. Ryder landed hard on the gravel while Axel's lunchbox burst open, scattering sandwiches, crisps and chocolate everywhere.

As Axel got down on his hands and knees to retrieve his sandwiches he realized the playground had suddenly gone quiet.

A dark shadow loomed over him. Looking up Axel saw a tall man in a black coat. It was so long it hung to his shoes and gave the impression that he floated over the

ground. His thin face was topped by black hair shining with oil. Everything about him was sharp – from his small pointed teeth to his narrow green eyes.

Axel knew without being told he was looking at Mr Batt, the head teacher. No wonder they called him the Vampire.

Mr Batt leaned down towards him. Without thinking Axel put a hand to his neck to protect himself.

CHAPTER 3
Staying Alive

"What is *this*?" demanded Mr Batt, pointing at Axel's lunch.

"Um ... a sandwich, sir..." said Axel. "Cheese and pickle."

"I can see that," breathed Mr Batt. "But what is it doing in my playground? In this school we do not tolerate *litter*."

Mr Batt spat out the word "litter" as if it was something nasty stuck in his throat.

Ryder pointed at Axel. "It was his fault, sir. He was swinging his lunchbox round and it burst open. I was just helping him to pick it all up."

"You big liar!" said Axel. "You were after my chocolate."

"Is this true, Ryder?" asked Mr Batt. "Did you try to steal this boy's lunch? A boy new to our school, if I'm not mistaken."

"No, sir," muttered Ryder.

Mr Batt bent down and fixed Ryder with a stare that seemed to hold the boy in a spell.

"I will ask you one more time. Did you try to steal from this boy?"

The colour drained from Ryder's face. "Yes, sir," he muttered.

Mr Batt pointed a bony finger at him. "Litter duty. I want to see this playground clean as a whistle. If I find one scrap, one speck, you will answer to me, Ryder. Understand?"

Ryder nodded his head, miserably. "Yes, sir." He darted a spiteful look in Axel's direction. Then he got down on his hands and knees and began searching for the tiniest scraps of litter.

Axel felt Mr Batt's cold hand on his shoulder.

"So you're the new boy, mmm?"

"Yes, sir. Axel Feinstein."

"Your head teacher tells me you're clever, Feinstein. Is that true?"

"I suppose so. I don't know, sir."

"Well, I don't have much time for cleverness, it gives children ideas, and ideas are a bad thing. At this school we like children to be quiet and tidy. Are you quiet and tidy, Feinstein?"

"Yes, sir," said Axel quietly. (It was hard to look tidy with a dirty sandwich in your hand.)

"Very well, you may go to your lessons. And remember…"

"Yes, sir?"

"'You do not drop litter in my school. Ever. Understand?"

Axel nodded. Mr Batt swept away with his black coat billowing out behind him. Axel wondered if the head was, well, off his head. Maybe he really was a vampire and haunted the school at night. Axel imagined him gliding silently through the corridors, thirsty for blood. He felt his neck again and shivered.

🐬🐬🐬

If Axel thought things couldn't get much worse, he was wrong. At Potter End things had been simple. He spent nearly all his lessons with Mr Crump in one classroom. At his new school he was handed a bewildering timetable where the day was divided into German, Science, Games, Maths, English and History. Each lesson was in a different part of the school and a bell rang every forty-five minutes. This was the signal for the class to jump to their feet and thunder off down the corridor to their next lesson. Axel tried to keep up but his legs were shorter than the others'.

Often a wave of children would appear and sweep him along in the wrong direction. If he ran, a teacher appeared in a door and barked at him: "No running in the corridor, boy!" He slowed to a walk and soon got lost again in the maze of corridors and stairs.

He was fifteen minutes late for his first lesson, which was German. Axel had never been taught German before and the only word he knew was goodbye (*Auf wiedersehen!*). The whole lesson was conducted in German and Axel sat in baffled silence.

Once the teacher asked him a question which sounded like *"Geshting kutz visor bish?"* "Goodbye!" he answered hopefully – but the class erupted with laughter.

He got so lost on his way to Science that he didn't arrive until the class were packing away.

Games was next, and by the time he found the sports block, the other boys had all changed into their kit.

"You're late, lad. Where's your kit?" asked the sports master, Mr Tucker.

"Um … I haven't got any, it's my first day," said Axel.

Mr Tucker pointed to a box in the corner, full of shirts and shorts.

"Borrow some from there and get changed quick."

"What are we doing?" Axel asked a boy as he stripped off his clothes and shivered.

"Rugby," replied the boy.

"Rugby?" said Axel. At Potter End they did ball skills and apparatus. He'd never played rugby in his life! He'd seen it once on TV and it looked like all-in wrestling.

The shirt he'd been given was so long it flapped down below his knees. He rolled up the sleeves so many times it looked like he was wearing water wings. When he emerged on to the rugby pitch, the rest of his classmates hooted with laughter.

38

It was raining and a gale seemed to be blowing across the pitch from the Arctic. Axel had taken off his glasses and could only see blurry striped shapes like a forest of moving trees.

The game started and the ball was thrown to Axel. He caught it and started to run towards the tall white posts as he'd been told. "Pass!" shouted someone. Axel tried to see who it was, but seconds later he felt like he'd been flattened by a herd of stampeding buffalo.

"Too slow! You should have passed," grumbled his team captain.

The game went on upfield while he checked to see if any bones were broken.

The next time the ball came his way, he tried to pass to someone else – anyone else really. "Here! Move it!" they cried. But the rugby ball was like a slippery eel. He juggled and caught it, before he was engulfed by the other team. This time they didn't bother to grab the ball, they just picked up Axel and carried him thirty metres before slamming him down on the muddy turf under the posts.

"Never mind the circus tricks," moaned Axel's captain. "Just pass it!"

"I'm trying!" groaned Axel, crawling out of a puddle. By the end of the game he had more bruises than a sack of rotten apples. He looked like a mud monster that had emerged from a swamp.

As they trooped off, Mr Tucker banged him hard on the back. "Don't worry, lad. You'll get the hang of it next time."

Axel groaned. He'd never survive a next time.

Lunchtimes were no safer. Axel noticed Ryder patrolling the playground with his gang, a dangerous look in his eye. He dodged round a corner to keep out of sight and found himself face to face with a group of girls leaning against a wall. They were all taller than him. A girl with curly red hair was painting her nails black.

"Looking for someone?" she asked.

"Not really," said Axel, turning pink.

"What's your name?"

"Axel."

"So where are your little pals, Axel?"

"I haven't got any. Not here anyway."

"Oh, that's sad! No friends," cooed the girl.

"Ahh! He's sort of cute," said another girl.

"Got a girlfriend, Axel?" asked the red-haired one.

Axel blushed deeper. "Er ... what?"

"A girlfriend. Don't tell me you haven't!"

"Well, not exactly..." stammered Axel.

"What about Debbie? She'll go out with you, won't you, Debs?"

The one called Debbie giggled. Axel thought she looked big enough to eat him.

"No, it's OK! I just remembered. I *have* got a girlfriend," Axel lied.

"Oh, you remembered! What's her name, then?"

"She's ... um ... she's called ... Trudy," said Axel with sudden inspiration.

"You wouldn't be making her up, would you, Axel?" asked the red-haired girl. "Because Debs would be upset. I think she *really* fancies you."

The three of them were coming closer, giggling and ruffling his hair.

"Sorry! I've got to go," squeaked Axel desperately, breaking away.

He ran across the playground. There seemed to be traps lying in wait around every corner. No one at Potter End asked if he had a girlfriend. Axel felt everything he said and did at this school was wrong. The letter had said he would be "better suited" to this school, but he felt like an alien from another planet.

He felt the curious sensation that someone was watching him and looked up. Mr Batt was standing at the window of his room, staring down on him. Axel shivered – the head teacher gave him the creeps.

CHAPTER 4
Rescue Plan

"It was only your first day," said Trudy. "It's bound to get better."

"It won't," said Axel hopelessly. "I know it won't. I hate it there."

They were walking home from school. Trudy had brought along Darren and Mae Li to try and cheer him up. But Axel was sunk in gloom. Trudy had never seen him look so miserable.

"Come on," said Darren. "The teachers can't be as bad as Crump."

"They're worse and I have dozens of them," said Axel. "A different one for every subject."

"Weird," said Mae Li.

"And you should see the head teacher," said Axel. "He's a vampire!"

"Axel! You're making it up," said Trudy.

"I'm not! He wears a long black coat and I bet he sleeps in a coffin at night. His name's Mr Batt and everyone calls him the Vampire."

"Doesn't he mind?" asked Darren.

"You don't say it to his face!" said Axel. "I only met him once and he scared me to death."

"What about your class? Didn't you make any friends?" asked Trudy.

"Not really. Well, only these girls..." Axel blushed, remembering the lie he'd told.

"Trudy," he said. "Can you do me a big, big favour?"

"How big?" said Trudy.

"Well, the thing is ... if anyone asks you,
can you say that you're my ... you know..."

"Your what?"

Axel took a deep breath. "My girlfriend,"
he blurted out.

Trudy stared
at him. She
swung her
schoolbag at
his head.
"AXEL!
Forget it!"

"OK, OK, I only asked,"
said Axel retreating under a hail of blows.
"It's just these girls kept asking who my
girlfriend was and I had to say something
so I said ... I said it was you."

"You *told them* I was your girlfriend?"

"What else could I say?"

Trudy swung her bag again. Axel dodged behind Darren who was doubled up with laughter. "Come on, you two," he soothed. "Kiss and make up now!"

Trudy's bag clouted him on the ear.

They walked on in silence for a while. Axel was deep in thought.

"Axel," said Mae Li. "You know you said you're the smallest in the school?"

"Yes?" said Axel.

"But you don't mean that. Surely *all* the children can't be taller than you?"

"All of them," nodded Axel.

"But isn't that a bit odd?" asked Mae Li.

"Yes," said Trudy. "There are lots of kids at our school smaller than you. Some of them are tiddlers."

"I've been thinking about that," said Axel. "And there's another thing too. Why's it called Hangem High?"

"That's the name," said Darren, brightly.

"I know, but shouldn't it be Hangem Junior or Hangem Primary, unless…"

"Unless what?" asked Trudy.

"Unless," said Axel, "it *isn't* a primary, it's a secondary school."

They all stopped in their tracks and stared at him.

"Come on!" said Darren. "You're only nine. Why would they send you to a secondary school?"

"Because he's so brainy!" said Trudy. "Axel's right. How could we be so thick? That's why they're all bigger than you. It's a secondary school!"

Axel kicked himself for not seeing it before. The letter hadn't spelled it out, and so he'd just assumed he was going to another primary. But the "higher level" the letter mentioned had meant secondary level. No wonder he didn't belong at Hangem High. All the other children were much older – some as old as sixteen! How could he ever hope to fit in? He'd always be the oddball, the little kid with the brains.

They'd reached the park. Little kids were laughing and playing happily on the swings and slides. Axel slumped on to the bench and rested his chin in his hands. Trudy, Darren and Mae Li came to sit beside him.

"You've got to help me," pleaded Axel. "I won't survive in there. You've got to get me out."

"Don't worry. We'll think of something," said Trudy. She was about to put an arm round him but then remembered she might look like his girlfriend.

They sat for a while, trying to think of an escape plan.

"Got it," said Darren at last. "Dynamite! We blow up the whole school. *Kaboom!*"

"Great, Darren. We get arrested and Axel gets killed in the explosion," said Trudy.

Darren shrugged. "Well, at least he wouldn't have to go to school."

Axel gave Darren a look.

"In films they always dig an escape tunnel," said Mae Li.

"I can't even find the way to my class," said Axel. "I'll never tunnel my way out. And anyway, they'd only send me back again."

"But what if they don't want you back?" said Trudy.

Axel looked puzzled. "How do you mean?"

"Well, what if you did something *so bad* that they'd have to expel you?"

Mae Li clapped her hands. "Yes! That's a great idea."

"Brilliant!" said Darren. "What's expel mean?"

"It means they throw me out," said Axel doubtfully. "But how do I get them to do that?"

"It's got to be something seriously bad," said Trudy.

"Put superglue on your teacher's seat," suggested Mae Li.

"Or a slug down the back of her jumper," said Darren.

"I could be late for every lesson," said Axel. "I'm good at that."

"Not bad enough," said Trudy. "What about the head – Count Dracula!"

"The Vampire?"

"Yes, he's the only one who can expel you," said Trudy. "You could do something to him. Something that makes him really mad."

Axel shook his head. "It's all right for you, you haven't met him. What if he really is a vampire? I could be murdered in my bed!"

Axel fingered his neck to check for tell-tale teethmarks.

Trudy shrugged. "OK, we're only trying to help. You can always stay at Hangem High, if you prefer."

"I can't," said Axel flatly. "I've got to get out."

Trudy wound a lock of hair round her finger, which was a sure sign she was thinking.

"Got it!" she said at last. "Here's the plan. It'll take a lot of nerve, but I think it'll work..."

CHAPTER 5
The Worst Crime

Mr Batt stood on the stage with his arms folded. His lizard eyes flicked from side to side, missing nothing. Below him the children filed quietly into the assembly hall and took their seats. Mr Batt watched them like a hawk, ready to swoop on anyone who spoke or sniggered. He was not in a good mood.

This morning he'd received his invitation to the Parents Association Fancy Dress Ball. It was an annual event, which he would gladly have missed. Mr Batt hated parties, and he hated dressing up in silly costumes even more. Besides he couldn't think what to wear. Last year his butler's costume had been a disaster – people kept handing him their coats as they arrived.

Almost all the classes were in now. Axel was seated near the back of the hall, trying not to think. If he let himself think he would lose his nerve. He tried counting backwards in odd numbers. He felt in his pocket again to check he'd got the vital equipment Darren had lent him. What was it Trudy had said? *Just do it. It will all be over in a few seconds.*

It was all very well for Trudy. She wasn't sitting where Axel was sitting, looking up at Mr Batt. The head teacher was scowling at the rows of children as if he suspected them of something. He didn't look to be in a good mood. When the time came to put his plan into action, Axel was sure he would be frozen to his seat.

The last class took their seats. Mr Batt approached the wooden lectern and rested his long white hands on it. He gazed down at the sea of anxious faces.

"This morning I wish to talk about a problem in our school," he said.

Axel felt his face go hot. Had he been discovered already?

"I am referring, of course, to the problem of *litter*," said Mr Batt. "Some children have developed the nasty habit of bringing litter into school. In their grubby little pockets. Some of you have nasty, dirty things in your pockets right now."

Mr Batt glared at his audience, who squirmed in their seats. Axel wondered if Mr Batt knew what he had in his pockets. Could vampires see through your trousers?

"This school is a tidy school," said Mr Batt. "That is why I have installed nine brand new bins in the playground. At breaktime every pupil will empty his or her pockets into these bins. Do I make myself clear?"

Mr Batt let his words hang in the silence. "We will now sing hymn number seventy-four."

The pupils breathed a sigh of relief and all reached for their hymnbooks. Axel knew it was now or never. Trying to ignore the thumping of his heart, he pushed his way to the end of the row.

It was a long walk up to the stage. To Axel it felt like he was walking towards the edge of a cliff. He could see Mr Batt on the stage and prayed he wouldn't look up from his hymnbook. As he passed each row children's faces turned to look at him in astonishment.

No one had ever dared to interrupt one of
Mr Batt's assemblies. "Go back," their faces
told Axel. "Sit down! Are you out of your
mind?" Closer and closer Axel
came to the stage. And
now the head teacher
glanced up and saw him.
His green eyes narrowed,
and his thin mouth twitched.

Axel wanted to run and hide,
but it was too late now. He had
to go through with it. He mounted the steps
one at a time as the singing faded away.
The piano carried on by itself, then tailed
off into silence. The whole school was
looking at the new boy, waiting to see
what he was going to do.

Axel felt in his pocket and put a hand
to his mouth. His hands were shaking.
He walked towards Mr Batt and came to
a dead stop. The head teacher glared down
at him furiously.

"Yes?"

"I wanted to ask you a question – sir," said Axel in a quavery voice.

"Speak up," said the head, his voice dangerously quiet.

"Yes, sir. Is it … is it true you're a vampire?"

Axel bared his teeth in a smile to reveal the set of plastic Dracula fangs he was wearing. There was a gasp from the front rows, followed by an awful silence. Surely the small boy on the stage was about to die a horrible death?

Mr Batt stared at Axel. He bent lower and lower, peering at Axel's plastic fangs. Then he parted his lips and a strange sound came out of his mouth. It was a sound no one in the school had ever heard before. Mr Batt was actually laughing.

Heh heh heh...

"Heh heh! Very good, Feinstein. Heh heh!"

"P-pardon, sir?" said Axel.

"A joke is it not? And just what I need for the Fancy Dress Ball. I shall go as a vampire. Vampire Batt. Heh heh! Now, back to your place, boy."

Mr Batt recovered himself and resumed his scowl. Axel turned away and left the stage, baffled. He was quite certain that Mr Batt was as mad as the moon. On a signal from the head, the piano started to play and the hymn was taken up as if nothing had happened.

Axel's plan had failed dismally. He had committed the most daring crime he could think of – speaking the headmaster's nickname in front of the whole school – but it had failed. He wasn't going to be expelled from Hangem High. He wasn't going anywhere.

CHAPTER 6

A Push in the Right Direction

At breaktime Axel joined the lines of children
emptying their pockets into the new bins.
Mr Batt had ordered nine wheelie-bins –
which looked like giant buckets on wheels.
This was a cunning device so they could be
pushed round the playground by anyone on
litter duty. Right now they were lined up so
that the whole school could file past them.

Crisp packets, tissues, old bus tickets, bits of string, mouldy sweets and chewed pencils were tossed into the bins. Soon all nine of them were filled almost to the brim. It was surprising how much rubbish collected in the pockets of eight hundred children.

Axel shuffled along, paying little attention – even when the others in the line started pointing at him.

"Hey, look who it is, Little Dracula!"

"Show us your fangs!"

"You're bonkers. Why did you do it?"

"I was trying to get expelled," replied Axel, truthfully.

"Ha ha! Good one. Trying to get expelled!"

Everyone around him laughed. They thought he was joking.

Axel reached the nearest bin and emptied his pockets. He didn't even bother to keep the pocket compass he'd got in a cracker last Christmas. Why would he need a compass? He wasn't going anywhere. For the next seven years of his life he was stuck at horrible Hangem High. In time his friends at Potter End were bound to forget him. Why should they care if he got trampled to death in a rugby match one day?

If Axel had paid more attention he would have noticed Ryder join the queue behind him. Ryder had spotted Axel. He hadn't forgotten how the new kid had got him in trouble with Mr Batt. Now at last he saw a chance to get his revenge.

Ryder pushed his way along the queue until he was only a few places behind Axel.

When Axel walked away from the bins, he felt a hand on his shoulder. He turned round to see Ryder.

"Hello, Shrimp."

Axel groaned. This was the last thing he needed.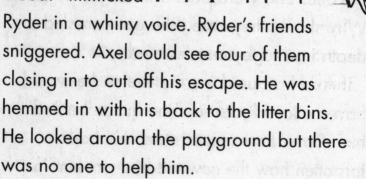

"Leave me alone," said Axel. "I'm not in the mood."

"He's not in the mood!" mimicked Ryder in a whiny voice. Ryder's friends sniggered. Axel could see four of them closing in to cut off his escape. He was hemmed in with his back to the litter bins. He looked around the playground but there was no one to help him.

"You've had it now," said one of Ryder's pals.

"We've been waiting for you, Shrimp."

"Say your prayers."

"There's no teachers to help you this time."

Axel looked up at the top window below the bell tower, but Mr Batt wasn't at his usual station.

Axel tried desperately to think of something. He thought of a film he'd seen once where a man flattened an army of spear-carrying guards using only his bare hands and feet. He raised his hands and moved them in slow circles.

"I warn you," he said, "I'm a master of kung fu."

"Don't. You're scaring me," said Ryder sarcastically. He came a little closer.

There was a moment like the stillness before a thunderstorm. Axel looked at Ryder and Ryder glared back at him. Then suddenly Ryder took a step forward and shoved Axel hard in the chest with both hands. Axel stumbled backwards.

"Go on, Ryder!"

"Squash the little pimple!" shouted voices.

Ryder came on and shoved him again, this time harder. Axel staggered back and collided with something heavy behind him. As he slid to the ground he saw the litter bin rock back and forwards on its wheels. Slowly – as if making up its mind – it toppled over and hit the next bin. This set off a chain reaction. Each bin toppled into the next like skittles going down in a bowling alley. Axel watched horrified as all nine bins hit the ground with a sound like cannon-fire.

WHUMP! WHUMP! WHUMP! went the bins.

Out spilled the crisp packets, tissues, bus tickets and paper from eight hundred pairs of pockets. The wind pounced on them eagerly and began to toss them round the playground like confetti.

Axel gazed in wonder at the mayhem he'd created in the space of a few seconds. All he'd done was fall over.
The odd thing was that no one was shouting or laughing.

Then Axel noticed the dark shadow
looming over him. Mr Batt was not at his
window – he had decided to come out and
inspect the progress of the pocket-emptying.
The sight that greeted him was a playground
that looked like a
rubbish tip, with litter
swirling and
dancing
in the
wind.

The head's
face was
deathly pale.
His thin lips
trembled
with anger.
Around his head the litter danced and
bobbed. Mr Batt reached out a hand and
caught a white paper bag that was drifting
by. He crumpled it in his fist. When he spoke
his voice was a whisper.

"Who?" he hissed. "Who *dared* to do this?"

Ryder gulped. He pointed at Axel.

Axel opened his mouth to protest his innocence, then snapped it shut again. Suddenly he knew what he had to do. A crazed smile spread across his face.

"It was me," he said. "Me! Me! I'm the litterbug! Ha ha! Hee hee!"

Gathering fistfuls of paper he threw them high in the air for the wind to take.

CHAPTER 7
Potter End

It was half-past ten on a Monday morning.
Mr Crump was writing the answers to the
spelling test on the board.

"Now," said Mr Crump, turning to face
the class. "Who got eighteen out of twenty?"

No one put their hand up.

"Seventeen?" asked Mr Crump.

"Sixteen? Fifteen? Fourteen?"

Still no one put their hand up. Mr Crump shook his head. "Hopeless," he said. "Your spelling is a disgrace. We'll have another test next week."

The class groaned. They hated Crump's Monday spelling tests. Darren Blott had only scored three out of twenty, and he'd been copying from his neighbour.

Just then there was a knock at the door.

"Come in!" said Mr Crump, breezily.

The door opened and in stepped Mrs Fudge, the head teacher. She was followed by a smiling Axel Feinstein.

"Mr Crump," said Mrs Fudge. "Look who's here."

Crump turned pale. He went to sit down on his chair and missed, ending up on the floor. "But ... but..." he stammered.

"Mr Batt phoned on Friday to ask if Axel could return to Potter End," explained Mrs Fudge. "He seemed most eager. And of course I said we'd all be *delighted* to have Axel back. Isn't that right, Mr Crump?"

Mr Crump was so delighted he seemed lost for words.

Trudy, Mae Li and Darren beamed at Axel. He'd told them he was being sent back and they'd been looking forward to his arrival. It was worth the wait, just for the look on

Crump's face. Their teacher looked as if a ghost had come back to haunt him.

As Axel made his way to his old seat at the back of the class, the class cheered and banged on their desks.

"All right, all right," grumbled Crump. He waited until Mrs Fudge had closed the door behind her, then he turned on Axel. "OK, Feinstein, how did you do it? How did you get yourself sent back in less than a week?"

Axel shrugged innocently. "I don't know, sir. I suppose I made a real *mess* of everything."

Young Hippo
**Terrific stories, brilliant characters
and fantastic pictures – try one today!**

There are loads of fun books to choose from:

Jan Dean
The Horror of the Black Light
The Terror of the Fireworms

Alan MacDonald
The Great Brain Robbery
The Great Escape

GHOSTLY TALES

Disastrous Dez

Penny Dolan
The Ghost of Able Mabel
The Spectre of Hairy Hector

Mary Hooper
Mischief and Mayhem!
Spooks and Scares!

Frank Rodgers
Head for Trouble!
Haunted Treasure!

Franzeska G. Ewart
Bugging Miss Bannigan